Cool Time Song

By CAROLE LEXA SCHAEFER • Illustrated by PIERR MORGAN

Viking

This one's for us . . . and the whole wide world.—Carole & Pierr

Viking

Published by Penguin Group

Penguin Young Readers Group, 345 Hudson Street, New York, New York 10014, U.S.A.

Penguin Books Ltd, Registered Offices: 80 Strand, London WC2R 0RL, England

First published in 2005 by Viking, a division of Penguin Young Readers Group

1 3 5 7 9 10 8 6 4 2

LIBRARY OF CONGRESS CATALOGING-IN-PUBLICATION DATA

Schaefer, Carole Lexa.

Cool time song / by Carole Lexa Schaefer ; illustrated by Pierr Morgan.

p. cm.

Summary: After a hot day on the African savannah, the animals begin to move and make sounds in the cool air of evening.

ISBN 0-670-05928-5 (hardcover)

Special Markets ISBN-13 978-0-670-06238-6, ISBN-10 0-670-06238-3

Not for Resale

[1. Savannah animals—Fiction. 2. Animals—Fiction. 3. Africa—Fiction. 4. Animal sounds—Fiction. 5. Nature conservation—Fiction.] I. Morgan, Pierr, ill. II. Title.

PZ7.S3315Cl 2005   [E]—dc22   2004012479

Manufactured in China   Set in Regula   Book design by Nancy Brennan

Sun rules the day.

It beats down so hard

on the dry land

that kudus and zebras
try to hide from its rays
in the thin shade
of thirsty acacia trees.
It bakes everything so long

that munching giraffes must
search and search the treetops
to find enough
tender unscorched leaves.

And elephants must crust themselves
with layer upon layer of dust
to protect their tough, thick skins.

Sun burns so very strong
that lion, *royal* lion,
sits weak as a cub
in the rising heat.

And hyena, *laughing* hyena,

lies still as a stick

in the stubbly grass.

But Earth turns.

Dusk comes.

And even Sun's fierce power

fades.

In that hour,
before lions begin to prowl,
or hyenas to follow their trail,

a calm, a peaceful,
a cool time
settles on the savannah.

In that time,
the animals—
all together—
make a song.

Kudus and zebras drum with their hooves—

Puh-tuh. Puh-tuh. Puh-tah.

Giraffes rattle dry leaves—

Shah-ticka.

Shah-ticka. Shah.

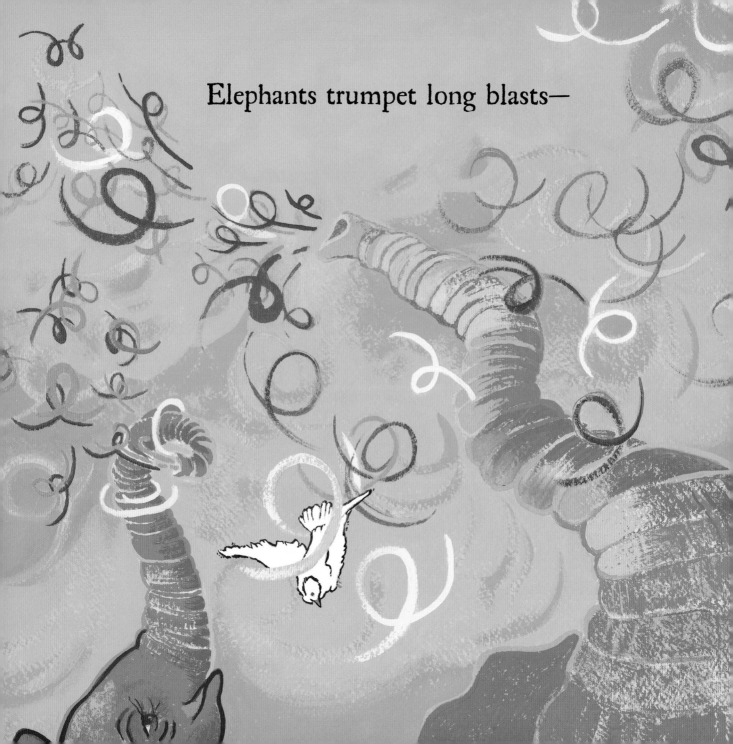

Elephants trumpet long blasts—

Vroo-oot. Vroo-oot. Vroo-eet.

Lions roar—

Grr-mrow-ool!

And hyenas howl—

Haroo-hee-hee. Haroo-hee-hee-hee.

Like heat, their cool time song rises.

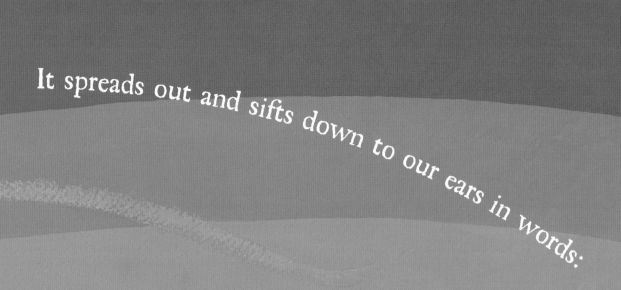

It spreads out and sifts down to our ears in words:

"Care for the water."

"Tend the land."

"Laugh together."

"Hear the animals'
peaceful cool time song."
"And, people, oh people—

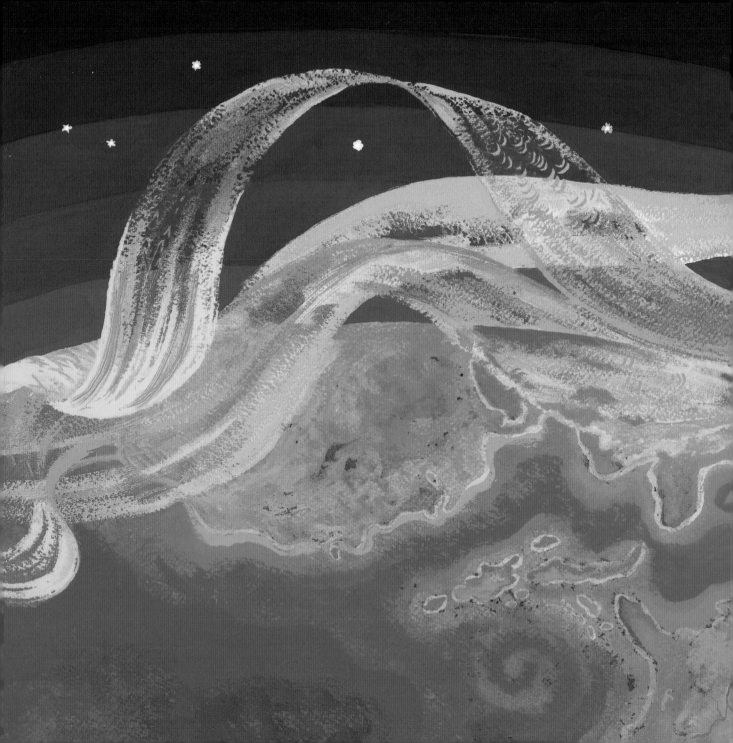

"sing along."